This Book Belongs To

_____

Centaworld Greetings, Inc.
5374 Highway 98 East
Destin, Florida 32541.

First Edition 1994 10 9 8 7 6 5 4 3 2

Library of Congress Catalog Card Number 94-67947
ISBN 0-9642321-0-3 Manufactured in the United States of America

The True Spirit of Christmas

Welcome to our world.
Welcome to Lavida. We are so glad you are here.
You are just in time to join us for our annual Christmas pageant.
Come with us now. Come into our world.

Bruce Bear stood back to admire the wreath he had just hung.

"That looks great, Bruce!" said his wife, Betty. She was busy stringing cranberries and popcorn for the Christmas tree.

"Freida Feline, will you stand still!" exclaimed Ophelia Otter. "I'm never going to finish this elf costume!"

Zeke, the town mayor, walked onstage, tugging at his Santa suit. "I don't know why this thing gets smaller every year," he muttered.

Mavis Mouse bustled about the stage, trailing bits of ribbon and pages of script behind her. "Three weeks!" she kept repeating. "Only three weeks until Christmas Eve. How will we ever be ready on time?"

The whole town of Lavida buzzed with excitement. This year's Christmas pageant was more important than ever before. Raphael Raton, director of the world-famous Mouseco Ballet, was coming to spend Christmas with his old friend, Mavis. Everyone agreed the pageant had to be perfect for Raphael's visit. They wanted Mavis to be proud of them.

Mavis clapped her hands loudly. "Okay, everyone, time for rehearsal. Choir, take your places."

When the choir was ready, Mavis raised her arms. "Now, remember, my dears, our pageant's title is 'The True Spirit of Christmas.' Let's hear that spirit in your voices."

Before Mavis could lower her baton for the first song, the theater door banged loudly. Francesca Feline raced across the stage. She failed to notice when she knocked over Betty's bowl, scattering cranberries everywhere.

"I'm here, Mavis! Wait for me, Mavis!" Breathlessly Francesca took her place in the choir. "I'm ready to sing!"

"Oh, Francesca!" Mavis shook her head in frustration. "You promised me if I let you be in the pageant, you would behave, and you would be on time for rehearsals."

"I know. I'm sorry. Please, please, Mavis, don't be mad! I really want to be in the pageant. I'll be good. I will. I promise I will."

Still shaking her head, Mavis tapped her baton. "All right, my dears. *Let's hear the spirit.*"

Francesca's voice rose above everyone's. She sang joyfully. She sang enthusiastically. She was totally off-key.

Mavis lowered her arms and tapped her baton. "Francesca, my dear, I can't hear anyone except you."

"Oh, thank you, Mavis," Francesca clapped her hands delightedly. "I just love Christmas songs!"

"Well, that's nice, dear. But I'd really like to hear the rest of the choir!"

"She especially needs to hear me!" sniffed Penelope Pigg, the lead soprano.

"Oh, I see. I'm sorry."

The choir sang again. Francesca tried to sing softly. But as the beautiful words of the song rose around her, she grew more and more excited. The more excited she grew, the louder she sang. Soon her joyful voice drowned out all the rest.

Mavis lowered her arms. The choir looked at Francesca, who smiled back at them.

Mavis cleared her throat. "Francesca, I realize you love singing. But I was thinking...we have lots of people in the choir. What we really need is another elf. Do you think you could be an elf?"

"An elf!" Francesca exclaimed, "Oh, yes, I'd love to be an elf! I'd be the best elf ever! Please, let me be an elf, Mavis!"

"All right. I think that might be best. Ask Ophelia to find you a costume. Tomorrow, you'll be an elf."

Betty Bear had finally gathered all her cranberries. She looked up just as Francesca raced across the stage.

"Oh, no!"

Cranberries rolled.

"I'm an elf! Ophelia! Where are you? I need an elf costume!"

Mavis shook her head and turned to the choir. *"Now with spirit!"*

The next day, Mavis called all the elves onstage. "Remember, elves, your job is to load Santa's sleigh. As you work, think about all the happy children who will open these presents. You are almost as excited as they will be on Christmas morning."

The stage door banged. Francesca ran toward Mavis, dropping her elf hat three times before coming to a breathless stop. "I'm here! I'm ready to be an elf!"

"Francesca!"

"I know, I know. I'm sorry. All the bells came off my hat, and they rolled under my bed, and I had to crawl under there to get them, and then I couldn't get them back on, and..." She paused for a breath. "I'll be good, Mavis. I will! I just love being an elf!"

Sighing and shaking her head, Mavis showed Francesca to her place. "Please, dear, do take it easy. Everyone ready? All right. *Now, with spirit!*"

The elves carried their packages to the sleigh and stacked them neatly.

Francesca picked up one box and walked carefully across the stage.

She trotted back.

She picked up two packages.

She skipped to the sleigh.

She ran back.

She picked up an armload.

She raced toward the sleigh.

She tripped over her sister Freida's curly-toed shoes.

Freida lost her balance, knocking over Hazel, Herbert, Henrietta, and Hank Hare. Elves and presents tumbled in every direction.

"Francesca!" Mavis was frantic. "What are you doing?"

Francesca looked up from the jumble of elf arms and legs and ears, giggling delightedly. "Oh, Mavis, I'm having such a good time! I just love thinking of those happy children opening these wonderful presents! I want to get Santa's sleigh loaded fast, so he can get going!"

"Oh, dear! I appreciate your excitement. But...well, I can see now that we just have too many elves. What we really need is another reindeer. Do you think you could be a reindeer?"

Francesca climbed from the elf pile and jumped to her feet. "Oh, yes, I'd love to be a reindeer. I'd be the best reindeer ever! Please let me be a reindeer, Mavis!"

"All right. I think that might be best. Find Ophelia and tell her you need a costume. Tomorrow you'll be a reindeer."

The elves had finally gathered their packages and untangled themselves. They looked up just in time to see Francesca racing across the stage.

"Oh, no!"

Elves and boxes tumbled.

"I'm a reindeer! Ophelia! Where are you? I need a reindeer costume!" Francesca shouted.

Mavis shook her head and turned to the jumbled elves. "Let's try again," she sighed, *"with spirit."*

The next day when the reindeer were ready for rehearsal, Mavis looked at them in silence. Then, she sighed and sat down. "I think we should wait a few minutes before we begin."

"Why, Mavis?" asked Baby Bear.

"You'll see," replied Mavis.

The reindeer looked at each other, confused.

Freddy Feline started to protest, "But, Mavis, we want to..."

The theater door banged. Francesca dashed across the stage, dragging her reindeer antlers. "Oh, good! You haven't started! I'm here, Mavis. I'm ready to be a reindeer!"

Mavis looked tired. "Put your antlers on, dear, and take your place."

Struggling with her antlers, Francesca tangled them with her brother Freddy's.

He pushed her. "Get away from me, Francesca!"

Baby Bear separated them.

"Can we please begin now?" asked Mavis. "Reindeer, your job is to prance across the stage. Think how important you are to Santa. You are eager for Christmas Eve to come so you can pull the sleigh. This is the night you live for, the one night of the year you get to do what you do best. *Let's see your spirit!*"

Francesca proudly took her place at the end of the line. The choir sang one of her favorite Christmas songs. She pranced to the music! She danced! She whirled! She twirled! She swirled around the stage. She closed her eyes, laughing with sheer delight.

Francesca didn't see the other reindeer prancing smartly back across the stage. She danced right into Freddy, tangling her antlers with his again.

Baby pranced into Francesca and Freddy. They all fell in a noisy heap of reindeer antlers and bells.

Prince Frog was right behind Baby. He tried to leapfrog over the pile. He didn't make it. He landed right on top, sitting on Baby's antlers.

"Francesca!" Freddy's voice came from the bottom of the reindeer heap. "You can't do anything right. You're going to ruin the whole pageant and embarrass Mavis in front of Raphael!"

Francesca took off her antlers. Slowly, she climbed from under the other reindeer. She stood up and looked at Mavis. Tears ran down her cheeks.

"I would never want to make you feel bad in front of Raphael. I just wanted to be part of the pageant. I wanted everyone to be proud of me for a change. But, Freddy is right. Everything I do is wrong. I'm sorry, Mavis."

The reindeer stood still as Francesca walked across the stage. No one looked at her. The theater door closed softly. Complete silence settled over the room.

Finally, Mavis turned to look at the reindeer. "All right, my dears," she said quietly, "straighten your antlers, and we'll try again."

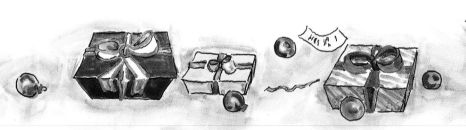

Then a strange thing happened. Something Mavis could not explain. Something no one in the pageant could understand.

Rehearsals began to go perfectly, just as they all wanted. *But something was missing.*

The choir sang in perfect harmony. *But something was missing.*

The elves loaded the sleigh perfectly. *But something was missing.*

The reindeer pranced perfectly across the stage. *But something was missing.*

After several days of perfect rehearsals, Mavis felt she was about to go crazy. She sat down beside Zeke in the front row. He was in his Santa suit, waiting for his turn to go onstage.

"I just don't know what to do, Zeke," Mavis said, almost sobbing. "Everything is perfect, and it's...empty. What is missing?"

The elves, the reindeer, and the choir members came to the front of the stage, waiting for Zeke's answer.

"Yes, tell us, Zeke. What can the problem be?" asked Penelope Pigg. "I know I am singing better than ever. *But something is missing.*"

Zeke looked at everyone for a moment before he said, "What is the title of the pageant, Mavis?"

"The True Spirit of Christmas," she replied.

"And what is the true spirit of Christmas?" asked Zeke.

"Well, it's about joy..." said Mavis.

"And excitement," said Baby.

"Enthusiasm," said Penelope.

"Giving," said Freida.

"Hope," said Prince.

"Love," said Freddy.

"You keep telling everyone to let you see the spirit, Mavis," said Zeke quietly. "But, who, more than anyone, really did show that spirit?"

They all looked at each other.

"Francesca!"

Mavis shook her head sadly. "Yes, you are right. We were so worried about making everything perfect, we forgot what our own pageant was about." She asked, "What can we do now?"

"I don't think Francesca will come back," said Freida. "She hasn't come out of her room since she left."

Freddy was about to cry. "I'm the one who made her leave."

"No, dear," said Mavis gently. "You just said what we were all thinking. All of us let her go."

Freddy stood up. "Well, she's my sister, and I shouldn't have been mean to her! I'm going to bring her back."

The theater door banged as Freddy ran for home.

At rehearsal next day everyone waited quietly, not knowing what to expect.

Finally Mavis said, "I suppose we should begin. Choir, take your places."

The theater door opened and shut softly. Everyone turned to watch as Francesca started slowly toward them. About halfway across the stage, she broke into a run. "Mavis! I'm here! Mavis, is it true? Do you really want me back? Freddy said you wanted me to be the Christmas angel! Can I, Mavis? Oh, can I really be the Christmas angel? I'd be the best Christmas angel ever!"

The choir members gasped and turned to stare at Mavis. She had always played the part of the Christmas angel herself. The Christmas angel put the star on the Christmas tree at the very end of the pageant. It was the most important part in the whole play.

Mavis thought for a moment. Then she smiled at Francesca. "My dear, we would be proud to have you as our Christmas angel."

It was Christmas Eve. Excitement filled the air of Lavida as Raphael Raton arrived. Everyone was anxious to get a look at him.

At the theater, the tension was thick. Francesca had pulled the Christmas tree down only twice in rehearsals. What would she do tonight?

As the curtain was about to rise, Mavis looked shaky. "All right, my dears," she said, *"remember the spirit."*

The pageant was beautiful.

The choir sang in spirited harmony.

The elves laughed and giggled excitedly as they loaded presents into the sleigh.

The reindeer jingled their bells merrily as they pranced across the stage.

Santa came onstage and took his place in the sleigh. "Ho! Ho! Ho! And away we go!" he shouted. All the children clapped and cheered.

It was almost over. The Christmas angel came onto the stage. She looked out at the audience. She waved just a little wave to her mom and dad.

Slowly she climbed the steps beside the huge Christmas tree. On the top step, she stood for a moment, holding the Christmas star.

Carefully, she reached out for the top of the tree.

She started to slide the star into place.

And she began to laugh joyfully.

Her laughter shook the star...

The star shook the tree...

The tree swayed...

The audience gasped!

Francesca tried to steady the tree, but she lost her balance. She grabbed the tree for support. Tree and angel toppled toward the stage.

"Baby, quick! Catch the tree!" shouted Freddy.

Baby dashed for the tree trunk. He used his reindeer antlers to help steady the huge trunk.

Freddy ran under the tree. "Don't worry, Francesca, I've got you!"

Francesca fell right on top of him. Her halo tangled in his antlers.

"Oh, Freddy, you saved me!" exclaimed Francesca. "You're the best brother ever! I love you!" And she gave him a great big Christmas hug.

For several moments no one moved. Suddenly in the front row, Raphael stood up and shouted, "Bravo!"

Then, everyone laughed and clapped and shouted with him.

Francesca unhooked her halo. She and Freddy helped each other up.

Other members of the cast moved beside them to take their bows.

Zeke brought a big bouquet of flowers to Mavis. "On behalf of the town of Lavida, we thank you once again for directing a spectacular Christmas pageant."

Mavis took the bouquet. Slowly, she pulled out one red rose. She turned to Francesca. "My dear," she said, "this is for you. You reminded us what the spirit of Christmas truly is."

Francesca took the rose. Timidly, she asked, "Mavis, do you think I could be the Christmas angel again next year?"

"You just might be," replied Mavis.

"But..." Francesca reached up and felt the dents in her halo, "my halo is all bent!"

"Yes, it certainly is!" laughed Mavis. "And we wouldn't have it any other way!"

We are so glad you came to visit our world. We hope you enjoyed our pageant. We would like to see you here again next year.

Until then, please come to visit soon. Come to visit often.

Paige West grew up in Shalimar, Florida and later received degrees from the University of Southern Mississippi and the University of Denver. For the past eight years she has taught sixth grade language arts and reading. While this is Paige West's first children's book, she has written many environmental education curricula and is co-author of the award winning *Heart of the Rockies*. Paige West now lives in Castle Rock, Colorado, with her cat, Zeke, and is working on several other children's books.

Paige West took great delight in introducing the world of Lavida, which is actually based on the real town of La Veta, Colorado. Francesca reminds her of many students she has known. In fact, Paige believes everyone has a little bit of Francesca in them.

Lyn G. Rackley was born and raised in Seattle, Washington. A graduate of Central Washington State University and Florida State University, she teaches art and design at Okaloosa Walton Community College. In addition to commission painting, Lyn works as a free lance illustrator, and has illustrated several books in the past. Lynn currently resides in Niceville, Florida, where she is busy creating a line of greeting cards for Centaworld Greetings, Inc. based on the characters in this book.

Lyn's work nurtures her inner self, and she is drawn to record her visual explorations on canvas or paper. She took great delight in revealing the character's personalities through her detailed, watercolor illustrations in "The True Spirit of Christmas."

Centaworld Greetings, Inc.
5374 Highway 98, East
Destin, Florida 32541